SUNSETS AND BAD BETS

MAISY MARPLE

ALSO BY MAISY MARPLE

Connie Cafe Series

Coffee & Corpses

Ligature & Latte

Autumn & Autopsies

Pumpkins & Poison

Death & Decaf

Turkey & Treachery

Mistletoe & Memories

Snow & Sneakery

Repairs & Renovations

Bagels & Bible Study

S'more Jesus

Proverbs & Preparations

Books & Bookings

Sharpe & Steele Series

Beachside Murder

Sand Dune Slaying

Boardwalk Body Parts

Fun in the Sun

Out to Sea

RV Resort Mystery Series

Campground Catastrophe

Bad News Barbecues

Sunsets and Bad Bets

Fun Foodie Mysteries

Burger & Dies

Died Shrimp

Ice Scream Sundae

Pastor Brown Series

O Holy Night

A Time to Repent

Trials of the Heart

Bite-Size Mystery

Christmas Murder in July

Dye-ing to Know

Short Stories

Forty Years Together

Long Story Short

The Best Gift of All

Miracle at the Mall

The Ornament

The Christmas Cabin

Cold Milk at Midnight

Coffee on Christmas

The Inn

Merry Little Christmas

Away in a Manger

A Christmas to Remember

Alone in the Woods

Short Story Collections

2021 Christmas Short Story Challenge

2022 Christmas Short Story Challenge

Addiction Help

Hard Truths: Overcoming Alcoholism One Second At
A Time

GET THREE FREE STORIES!

Click the banner to get three free stories!

1

The gentle breeze blew through Dan and Molly's bedroom window, rousing Dan to wake.

It was good to be home, in his bed, in his house. Here, he had room to move around and never had to worry about anyone bothering him.

He and Molly lived on a five-acre parcel of land on the outskirts of Auburn, New York. They had gotten used to the quiet life, even when they were working. That quiet gave them peace. It gave them time together, and it gave them time to reflect.

After they'd retired, they found that they had too much time to reflect and too much time alone with each other. They needed something more than five acres and a house.

That was when Molly saw an ad for Baldwin Beach RV Resorts. She'd suggested that they take a drive and check it out. After all, it wasn't that far from their home. A mere forty-five minutes. No problem.

Love at first sight, was, perhaps, a little too strong a term to describe how that first visit hit the two of them — but not by much. They were shown a site that was for sale, and they bought it on the spot.

It had been the first time in their marriage that they'd made a purchase over five hundred dollars without sleeping on it and giving it time to sink in. They had been as impulsive as a couple of kids at an ice cream stand trying to figure out what they wanted. Like the kids at the ice cream stand when the server came to the window and asked them what they wanted, Dan and Molly had been swept up by the emotion of it all and agreed to sign the contract and buy the place.

It was an exciting time in their life, and their years of planning had left them as they decided to set sail on the winds of whimsey.

They'd enjoyed the place a great deal. There was always something interesting to do and people to get to know. They had contests and access to the beach.

The only problem that they'd experienced since moving into their site a few months earlier was the dead bodies that had shown up. Of course, Dan being a retired cop, was not able to ignore this massive problem that had found its way into their laps.

After the last adventure they had, with two murders surrounding a barbecue competition, Molly suggested that they go home for a month and just enjoy some quiet.

Dan had agreed, and they locked up their camp and left without telling a soul.

It had been a great idea, and they'd loved the solitude of their lonely home on a five-acre parcel.

But as the breeze tickled Dan's nose, and he began to stretch his feet and wiggle his toes, there was something pulling at him that he hadn't felt since they'd come back home.

He needed to get out.

And he knew that was going to spell trouble for him and Molly.

D an decided to go for a walk and see if he couldn't clear his head. He and Molly both knew they needed to go back and close up their camp for the year, but when they'd left after the last set of murders, their future at the resort was very much up in the air.

Molly had come home and went on for days about how they should sell the place to somebody else. She'd sat at their table for hours, staring out into space, beating herself up for their impulsive decision. She'd poured through her bible, trying to find answers, wondering if, perhaps, their impulsive purchase had fallen under God's definition of folly.

"Did we bring it on ourselves, Dan?" She asked

one day when Dan had come in from mowing the
lawn to grab a sandwich for lunch.

"Bring what on ourselves?"

"The wrath of God? I swear, it's like we have a
big black cloud over our head as soon as we bought
that place."

"The wrath of God?" Dan was shocked to hear
his wife speaking like this. "No. It's nothing like that.
We just need to take some time and catch our breath.
When we go back, it'll be better."

Dan couldn't help but remember that conversation and many others like it that had come his way
over the course of the last few weeks.

As he reached the kitchen, the smell of coffee
touched his nose and tugged him toward the coffee
maker in the corner. The nice coffee maker they
owned was here, and Dan had forgotten how much
he liked being able to set a timer for his morning
coffee to start percolating. It added an extra layer of
enjoyment to waking up in the morning!

The coffee maker at the camp was a cheapie. It
got the job done, but Dan was usually making his
coffee with sleep remnants in his eyes, which was not
nearly as fun as just heading for the kitchen, grabbing
a mug, and pouring!

He grabbed a travel mug that he could take with
him on his walk and filled it up with hot, black dark

roast. The complexity and bitterness of it as it washed over his tongue was an absolute treat he looked forward to each and every day. It was amazing to him how something that simple brought him such joy. He'd experienced that feeling every day for the last forty years of his life. Waking up and having a cup of black coffee. He never deviated from it.

Yet, as he looked out over the back deck and into the woods that surrounded his property, he found himself wondering why he couldn't be content with the view that he'd stared at every day for the past twenty-five years. It made no sense to him that he could enjoy something as trivial as a cup of coffee, yet the property he and his wife had bought, paid for, and maintained all these years somehow became dull and boring.

Stepping out into the summer heat, he took a breath and another sip of coffee and set off to walk the trails, hopeful that he could figure out what was wrong with him.

3

Molly woke up alone and rubbed her hand across the crisp and cool sheet that had been Dan's spot until just an hour earlier. She could tell that he'd been up for a while because it was no longer warm from the heat of his body. He was no doubt walking in the woods with a cup of coffee and his thoughts.

She hoped that he was sorting things out. The first few weeks they'd been home, he seemed to be completely at peace, and Molly was hopeful that the rest of their days might end up feeling like that. However, lately, he'd been restless. He hadn't said anything to her about it, but she could tell. He'd started waking up earlier and earlier. His sleep was uneven, and he'd kicked her in hers more than she cared to think about.

Before she got up for the day, she decided to pick up her phone and get on her social media page. She scrolled absentmindedly as she ignored political posts and opinions from friends and family that she didn't really want to engage with at that moment. Then she saw something that snapped her out of her stupor.

In the middle of her screen was a post from Baldwin Beach RV Resort. They were having a poker tournament with a cash prize of one hundred thousand dollars for the winner.

As much as she'd been thinking about selling the RV they'd bought, all of those thoughts were set aside when she thought about herself and Dan playing high-stakes poker. They'd never played in a big tournament, and certainly never for that much moola. But they used to host poker games when Dan was on the force. The two of them couldn't be beaten, and oftentimes it was just him and her left standing at the end of the night.

She took a screenshot of the post and then took a deep breath before sitting up on the edge of the bed.

Maybe one more weekend at the resort park for a fun few days of poker was just what Dan needed to snap out of his funk.

She could give that to him, at least.

4

"Really," Dan raised an eyebrow at the news that Molly delivered promptly upon his returning from his walk. "And you'd be interested in doing something like this? I thought you were done with that place?"

"Well, I'm not super keen on going back given what we've been through, but we are quite the poker players. And you have to admit, we could have some fun with that much money. We could go on all sorts of different vacations that would spice up our retirement. And just think, if we sold off our camp, we could have an even bigger pile of cash to travel with."

Dan mulled this over as he sipped what was left in his travel mug. The idea was enticing. His retirement was more than enough for them to live on comfortably. They didn't want for anything. Molly's retirement was significantly less, but combined, they were able to treat themselves to some of life's little adventures.

But the thought crept into Dan's mind that if they were able to win the tournament and sell their campsite, then they might be rolling out of there with a quarter million in liquid cash. They'd be able to set aside a healthy inheritance for their daughter and grandchildren if they were ever blessed enough to have them. And that would leave the rest for them to go experience the world with. They could fly all over the place, take long cruises, and eat the finest food.

He had to admit, the idea was enticing to him, and he could tell by the look in Molly's eyes that it was enticing to her as well.

Without giving it much more thought than that, he nodded and said, "Alright, let's do it. We'll get our bags packed and be on the road by noon."

"Deal," Molly nodded.

There was something in the back of their minds that didn't quite feel right about this, but it was just too much money and opportunity not to go after because as a famous athlete once said, "You miss one hundred percent of the shots you don't take!"

5

The drive into Baldwin Beach was quiet. Neither Dan nor Molly knew what to say to each other. This whole RV experiment had been a terrible failure thus far.

Sure, they'd met some really nice people — people they would even call friends. Unfortunately, they'd been witness, or near enough, to three deaths in the past few months. Not to mention, their best friend seemed to be Officer Sherry of the Baldwin Beach PD. It just wasn't what they'd envisioned their retirement being.

Molly had thought that she would be free to spend her days on the beach or around the pool, reading clean romance novels and watching cheesy romcoms all night long. She figured that Dan would be by her side for a lot of it but would also go find his own things to do — things that wouldn't involve him being shot at.

Dan, on the other hand, didn't know what he was expecting from retirement. He'd hoped that he wasn't going to be getting shot at or dealing with criminals. So far, that box had yet to be checked. He had managed to sleep in past seven a few times, which was nice. But he'd lived a regimented life for so long that it was hard for him to get away from it. Since he was a little boy, he'd always been on the go and had to be tinkering or keeping his mind and body busy in some way. Lounging on the beach, or by the pool, or sitting down for a movie as the sun went down just wasn't fulfilling. He'd made an honest effort to make himself the husband that Molly had wanted in their retirement years, but he just couldn't shake enough of who he was to make it happen.

He knew that they had to get away from the RV resort, but he wasn't convinced that any other place on earth would be enough to satisfy the two of them, as they seemingly wanted such different things. They were going to have to figure it out, one way or the other. And he knew they would. They'd been together too long not to. They'd been through rough, unsettled waters in their marriage before. This was just the latest, and Dan knew that holding on for dear life and giving it up to the Lord might be the best way to deal with it.

Molly felt the same way.

That was the place they could start. It had always worked well for them in the past. The place where they had common ground always worked as the best jumping-off point. From there, prayer, patience, and persistence were the things that were going to guide them where they needed to go.

"Well, I didn't think we were ever going to see you two back here." Richard, their ninety-five-year-old neighbor, walked deliberately across the twenty-foot lawn that separated his camper from Dan and Molly's.

Molly walked into the camper, her pillow and a bag of groceries in hand. Dan shrugged and put their suitcase down. "We weren't sure, either. We both have a lot of thoughts about our future here."

Richard nodded somberly. "I understand. You know, back when Brenda and I got our place here, it was peaceful. Somedays, it was so quiet you could hear your own heart pumping the blood around in your brain. A lot's changed since then. Truth be told, we're probably just sticking it out at this point because we're too old to do anything else. And by golly, there's nobody in this place that's going to push us out of our place."

Dan admired Richard. He was such a good man. There was part of him — a big part — that wished he'd known Richard as a younger man. Dan could easily see them as friends in another life. As it was, he and Molly were just the latest neighbors that Richard and Brenda had to deal with. Of course, they did it with grace and love. But Dan knew they would never be close, and with the thoughts that he and Molly both had going through their minds, this weekend might be the last time they ever saw Richard and Brenda for the rest of their lives.

It was a sobering thought but a very possible reality.

This latest trip to the park felt like a mission to go win some money and get out. Nothing more. Nothing less.

"We're really just here for the poker tournament," Dan admitted. "Honestly, between you and me," he leaned in close, "I don't know how long we're going to be here. After the last few months, we are both having big-time second thoughts about this place."

Richard nodded his head and shrugged. "I can't say I blame you. If Brenda and I were your age and had been here only a few months, we'd probably be having the same conversation." He patted Dan on the shoulder and said, "You have to do what's best for you and your family. If that means you have to leave, then you have to leave. Don't worry about any of us. We'll be fine."

"Thanks, that means a lot."

With that, Richard turned around and began his slow and steady walk back to his site.

Before Dan could turn toward the door of his place, the sight of a police cruiser caught his attention.

You've got to be kidding me, he thought. *We just got back, and already the police are here.*

Officer Sherry pulled off to the side of the narrow road and parked his cruiser behind Dan and Molly's vehicle.

Stepping out, Dan noticed that he looked tired. Dan knew the feeling. He'd worked many a shift without so much as a wink of sleep going into them.

"I was starting to think you were never coming back!" Sherry said as he approached, a wide smile on his face.

"Join the club," Dan shrugged, glancing over at Richard and Brenda's site. "They didn't think we were coming back, either. Heck, we didn't even think we'd be back."

"Well, I can't say as I blame you." Officer Sherry put his hands on his hips and surveyed the surrounding area. "This place has seen its share of excitement for the year. I was talking to Skip and Tina the other day. They said they'd never seen anything like what's been going on here in all their days."

"Is something else going on?" Dan raised an eyebrow. "I've never seen you over here just driving around without something going awry."

"No," Officer Sherry shook his head. "Nothing like that. I talked it over with the guys at the station and management here, and we all decided that it might be a good idea if I did a drive-by around here three or four times a day. I feel a bit like Big Brother in 1984 if you ask me, but if it keeps the crime down for everyone, I guess it's a good thing."

Dan furrowed his brow. "I guess I don't have any better suggestions, but I have to believe that it makes it awfully hard for some people to relax, knowing that there's police presence here as often as it is."

"Yeah, it's not ideal," Sherry nodded. "I wish it were different, too. But you know, you can't have a free society without a moral one. Up until a few months ago, this place seemed to be a moral society of sorts. Either that, or they were just better at hiding their crime."

The two men shared a chuckle over that.

Just then, Molly stepped out onto the patio.

"Oh," she said, less than inviting. "Hello, Officer Sherry."

Sherry put his hands up in the air. "I swear, I'm not doing anything that's going to put your husband in harm's way. We're just catching up. That's all, promise."

She raised an eyebrow. "Well, if that's the case, would you like to join us for lunch? We were just about to grill some burgers and dogs. We have some chips and diet soda."

Officer Sherry glanced at his watch and then took a quick glance around. "If you don't mind, that sounds absolutely wonderful. I'm starving."

"Dan," Molly said. "You're grilling."

"I figured."

With that, Molly stepped back into the RV, leaving Dan and Officer Sherry to the cooking.

8

After Dan had grilled up a package of store-bought hamburgers, he and Officer Sherry sat down at the outside table. Molly grabbed herself a plate and then headed back inside.

She didn't have anything against Officer Sherry, and she was sure that her leaving the two men to themselves probably seemed like she was being a little curt on purpose. Perhaps, she was. However, the idea that they'd been back for less than an hour and Officer Sherry was already on their doorstep having lunch gave Molly a bad feeling. It felt like a sign that they needed to be anywhere but here.

Sitting at the kitchen table, she absentmindedly bit her way through her burger, shoving the occasional chip in her mouth as she stared out the window of the camper, out into the neighbor's patio. A cheesy romance novel was sitting next to her plate, and she had had every intention of reading it once they'd settled in and gotten reacquainted with the place.

But now, she couldn't get herself to focus on anything except the cloud that kept hovering over them. Coming back hadn't felt right when they were in the car on the way over, and now that they were, it felt worse.

Perhaps, she was being unfair. Perhaps, she was being unreasonable. Perhaps, Dan was capable of setting boundaries with Officer Sherry, and all of this worrying that Molly was doing was all for nothing. Maybe, everything was going to be just fine, and things would go well enough for them to continue to stay here.

But she had an uneasy feeling. Dan had always told her that her uneasy feelings were really just worries that took away from the joy of the day. He was keen on pointing out to her that none of her bad feelings ever resulted in anything terrible happening. They were just fear. Dan had heard a radio show host once say that fear was nothing more than false evidence appearing real. He'd taken that acronym and applied it to his own fears. Every time he brought it up with Molly, however, she'd thought he was neglecting her feelings.

Though, as she sat back now and thought about it, the last bite of burger riding her tongue from one part of her mouth to the other, she thought that Dan might've been right all those years.

But she was right this time…she just knew it.

9

While Molly was inside stewing about her fears and issues with Brennan Beach RV Park, Dan was having a lovely lunch with Officer Sherry.

The two sat down and enjoyed building really high double cheeseburger sandwiches on their plates and then piling them high with chips. They washed it all down with a couple of ice-cold cans of root beer.

"So," Dan asked, "what do you know about this poker tournament?"

"I know I'll be there," Officer Sherry nodded, then swigged a sip of his drink to wash the food out of his mouth. "I'm honestly surprised that Tina and Skip are going through with it given what's happened here this summer, but they said the risk of what might happen if they didn't hold the tournament was much worse. I guess they're approaching this as the lesser of two evils."

"Interesting," Dan mused. "Well, Molly and I are back for the tournament." He sat back for a moment, thinking. "I don't know. I don't know if it feels like the right move to be back here. What do you think?"

Officer Sherry shrugged. "You gotta be somewhere, right?"

"Yeah, I guess. It's just, home seems like a somewhere that might be safer. You know?"

Officer Sherry nodded. "That I do. But, you don't have much of a chance to win a hundred grand sitting on your keister at home, do you?"

"That's a good point you bring up. I just hope it's worth it."

"Well, you'll know soon enough." Officer Sherry looked at his watch. "It starts in five hours. I've got two more drive-throughs to do before I come over for that. I hate to eat and run, but I've got to go, or I'll never get my work done on time. Thanks for the burger!"

"I fully understand. We'll see you over there tonight."

Sherry stood up and made his way to the cruiser,

and Dan remained seated, wondering if he and Molly were just fooling themselves about their odds of winning the jackpot.

10

The rest of the afternoon passed without Dan or Molly saying much of anything to each other. They'd had a bunch of discussions over the past month about this place while they were at home with nothing much to do. Dan had heard all of Molly's issues with things, and Molly had heard Dan groan on and on about how life in retirement was too boring and stagnant for him.

She'd encouraged him to take up a hobby or join a men's group at church…anything that would fill the void of his career in law enforcement.

Hobbies weren't exciting enough.

All the men's group wanted to do was sit and talk and sing and eat. Not that there was anything wrong with that, but after a few meetings he'd quickly lost interest. He was a doer, and the local men's group at his church didn't really seem to want to *do* anything of note.

Dan walked for hours on end in the woods. That was what he did. He walked around town, always on the lookout for a way to help. He walked around the house, wondering if there was anything he could do to help Molly. Most of the time, the answer was no. And on the occasion that it was yes, it was typically something mundane, like popping the top off of a pickle jar or reaching for something on a high shelf that she couldn't get to.

Molly was becoming frustrated with Dan as well. She couldn't seem to get him to be content with what he'd worked his whole life for. They could have gone for long walks at all sorts of scenic parks around their area, but that wasn't exciting enough for him. They could have gone to visit friends and relatives they hadn't seen in years, but he wanted to stay close to home just in case. Just in case what, he never said. Deep down, she thought that her husband viewed himself as their own private security firm, determined to stay around the house in which he felt trapped in order to keep it safe from harm. She could see that he was becoming depressed, and she desperately wanted to help him.

Perhaps that was why she suggested this tournament. They'd both played poker years ago, and had been quite good. In fact, they'd been good enough to probably win a big sum of money when they were younger. She was hopeful that playing poker was like riding a bike. After a few hands, they'd both be analyzing their opponents, watching them call, raise, bluff, hold, and fold.

Did they really have a shot at winning the money? Naw. She knew the answer was *naw.* But she also knew that Dan needed more than he was getting sitting at home.

So, she did the thing she hated in hopes that it would raise his spirits. She brought them back to the RV resort, and now the two of them were barely speaking to one another.

They were each grateful when the clock on the microwave read 7:30 that evening. That meant it was time to go play poker and get their minds off of how badly each of them were communicating with each other about their true feelings, and how they were going to be able to come to some sort of agreement about what the rest of their lives were going to look like.

Hopping in the golf cart, they drove back to the field that had been the source of so many interesting memories for them, hopeful that the ones that would be made during the tournament would be enough to give them both some level of hope about anything.

11

Word had certainly gotten around about all of the shenanigans that had taken place over the past few months at Baldwin Beach. There were tables and chairs set out for easily double the number of people who had braved the treacherous paths with their golf carts and decided to throw their hats in the ring for the big prize.

Molly and Dan, along with Officer Sherry, were among them. Tina stood at a long table at the side of the field with a clipboard in front of her. She had a smile on her face, as per usual. However, as they approached to sign in for the poker tournament, Dan and Molly could sense that there was less sunshine behind her grin.

"Hey, you two!" Tina ran around the table and gave Molly a death grip of a hug and then turned to Dan and gave him one as well. "It's been so long. Where have you two been?"

"Home, mostly," Dan replied.

Molly nodded. "That's about the size of it."

Skip walked past Tina. She reached out her hand and grabbed his arm. "Skip, look who's here! It's Dan and Molly!"

Skip eyed them with his usual motionless features. "Well, isn't that hunky dory. If you give me just a moment, I might muster up the strength to do a cartwheel as a way of demonstrating my excitement."

Tina released her grip and slapped him on the arm. "Be nice. That's not how we greet our guests who have come back to play for a chance to win big."

Skip stopped and turned to face them directly. "Please forgive me. I can't move my arms, and my head hurts. I set up all of these tables because someone said we were going to have a bigger turnout than usual." He gave Tina a snide look. "Plus, I haven't eaten a thing all day."

"Now, that's your fault," Tina defended herself. "You could have stopped long enough to sit down and have a sandwich, you knucklehead."

Skip shrugged. "Well, I'm going to go home and have one now. How's that grab ya?"

Without waiting for a response from any of them, he continued walking toward his pickup truck, which was parked behind the grandstand of the field.

"Oh, don't think a thing about him," Tina guffawed. "He's just a sour puss who hasn't learned how to take care of himself yet. Between you and me, I'm starting to think he's never going to get there."

Molly and Dan each gave a pacifying smile and signed in on the clipboard.

Tina then directed them to a table that seemed to be smack dab in the middle of everything. Dan sat on the side facing the grandstand, and Molly grabbed a chair next to him.

There was a man sitting across from them. He looked older than they were but not too far past them. He was heavy-set and wore a tank top and shorts. His arms were red from sunburn, as was his face.

"I haven't seen you around here," he said when Dan and Molly had settled in. Half standing up, he extended his hand. "Name's Bill. If you ever need a quick trim on your lawn, I'm your man. I used to teach public school, but between you and me, the sound of the lawn mower engine and the bites from the mosquitos aren't nearly as annoying as other people's children." He slapped a woman sitting next to him on the arm. "This is my wife, Sandra. She's still grinding away at her career. She teaches eighth graders how to write sentences because apparently the elementary teachers and parents of these kids couldn't get them to figure out how those blasted words work." He laughed.

She didn't.

Sandra looked to be about as thrilled to be sitting at the table with her husband as the students who had once attended Bill's classes when he was teaching. She took a long, deliberate, and almost unceasing drag off a cigarette. There was a full pack of them beneath a half-consumed package sitting on the table next to a lighter and what appeared to be a glass filled just below the brim of hard liquor.

"You'll have to excuse Bill. He used to teach history. I don't know how many history teachers you've ever met, but there seems to be something about their kind that believes social graces don't apply to them. It's a pleasure to meet you."

"Likewise," Molly returned. "This is my husband, Dan, and I'm Molly. We're relatively new here."

"Wait a minute," Bill sat up and leaned on the table. He rested his chin on his hands and stared hard at Dan. "I've seen you before. Were you, by any chance, up on that grandstand with Officer

Sherry a few months ago, telling everyone to stop spreading rumors about things that happen here in the park?"

Dan's face flushed, and before he could answer, Bill snapped his finger and wagged his finger in Dan's direction. "I thought you looked familiar." He gave his wife another swat on the arm. "You remember that, hon? Remember this guy and that Officer Sherry telling everyone to mind their own business." He sat back and had a healthy laugh over the memory of that day.

Dan didn't like him one bit. And upon the first few words that were spoken between them, had already made up his mind that he would never ever ask Bill to mow his lawn.

"You want a beer or something?" Dan asked Molly, ignoring Bill's comments.

"A glass of white wine would be lovely," she replied.

Dan stood up and headed to the bar that was set up over by the sign-in table. There was a decent line formed, but standing in line with total strangers seemed like the best bet he could make, given the fine folks they'd been paired up with.

If he could, he had decided he was going to see if Tina would be able to get them moved to a different table for the night. If she couldn't, then Dan and

Molly would have to make quick work of Bill and Sandra and send them home packing for the night.

Just as Dan was reaching the line at the bar, Tina came flying out of the main office for the park, across the road from the poker tournament.

"The money's all gone!"

12

W hat started as a small murmur of whispers and gasps, soon became a full-throated chorus of questions and accusations.

Who would do such a thing?

Where could the money be?

I bet it was this one…

No, it was most certainly this one…

While people were having conversations at their own tables, Molly looked over to the bar where Dan had been waiting in line. Dread filled her whole being when she saw that he had *that* look in his eyes.

He was already scanning over the crowd, moving his eyes from side to side, looking for any suspicious behavior that would inevitably arise from an announcement that a hundred grand worth of prize money had suddenly disappeared without any explanation.

Officer Sherry was on the move, walking past the tables of jilted poker players and over to where Tina was standing in tears. She'd hardly moved a step from where she'd made the announcement moments earlier.

When Dan saw Officer Sherry, he too made a beeline for the registration office where the money was supposed to have been housed for the evening.

He arrived just in time to hear Officer Sherry tell Tina that they should head back inside and lock the doors so they could talk about things privately.

"I've already seen this rumor mill in action," Sherry scoffed, gesturing to the gathered. "We need to keep this as buttoned up as possible."

But the news was out, Dan thought. Keeping this one buttoned up was going to be a far bigger challenge than any of them could have possibly anticipated.

13

———

Tina sat down in her office chair behind her desk and stared vacantly off into space. Officer Sherry took a seat in a chair on the other side of the desk that was typically reserved for new lot renters in the park. Dan quickly noted that he and Molly had sat in that seat when they'd signed their paperwork for the rental lot in the park a few months earlier.

Boy, had Tina looked a different sight then. She had been chipper and upbeat, competent and on top of everything. Even before they signed up for their rental lot, Dan and Molly had felt some trepidation and doubt. It was actually their face-to-face with Tina that had sealed the deal for them. They had been so taken with her positive energy and happy-go-lucky spirit that they figured it was the right thing to do.

Now, she was sitting slumped, her head in her hands, shaking back and forth and sobbing. She looked like they had felt so many times over the past few visits to their RV. The crime and lack of control around here had finally, it seemed, gotten to the one truly bright spot of the whole place.

"When was the last time you saw the money?" Officer Sherry said, taking a notepad from his pocket and grabbing a pen from Tina's desk.

"I don't know. Probably an hour or two ago. It was just before I went outside to set up the sign-in table and make sure that everything was set up to be perfect for the night." That phrase, *perfect for the night*, hung in the air for a few seconds, giving everyone an uncomfortable flutter in their stomachs. Things were certainly not perfect now, and they all knew it.

Officer Sherry glanced over at Dan and the two locked eyes. They knew they were going to be in for another mystery here. It was a feeling that brought no joy to Dan, and the feeling of Molly clinging to his arm so tightly he didn't ever think she'd let him go, was yet another reminder that she was not going to be pleased with the things he was probably going to have to do to bring peace and justice to this place, yet again.

"Where do you keep the money for big events like tonight's poker tournament?" Officer Sherry proceeded with his questioning.

Tina pointed to a small, square safe in the corner of the office. It was behind her desk and to the left of where she was sitting for anyone looking at her from straight ahead. Officer Sherry noticed that it was open, and except for a few official documents in a plastic sheet protector, it was empty.

"And exactly how much money did you have in that safe?"

"One Hundred Thousand Dollars," Tina whispered. "It was the exact amount of the prize money for the tournament. It was in ten separate envelopes, with one hundred hundred dollar bills in each of them."

Officer Sherry jotted this information down as Dan looked around the room. Sherry glanced at Dan and then followed his eyes up toward the corner ceiling in the back of the room. He nodded, knowing exactly what Dan was looking at.

"Do you have any security cameras in this office?"

"Yes," Tina nodded, pointing to the same corner Dan had been staring at for several minutes. "There's one there, and then there's another one on the outside corner of the building."

"Is there any chance that the one in the corner has an eye on that safe?" Sherry asked.

Tina's shoulders slumped. "No. It doesn't."

"Would it give us visual confirmation of the people who were in this building between the time you set up the tables and the time the money went missing?"

Taking a deep breath, Tina stood up and walked over to the camera in question. She stood on a nearby chair and did some fiddling in the back of it. Within five seconds, she stepped down from the chair and handed a very thin card to Officer Sherry.

"That's the SD card that we use to record. It gets wiped daily, and the rest of the footage is then uploaded to our cloud storage, but I don't have access to the online password. That's way over my security clearance."

"Can we plug this card into that computer?" Sherry nodded toward a laptop on Tina's desk.

Tina smiled. "As a matter of fact, we can."

an, Molly, and Officer Sherry gathered around Tina as she slid the card into the side of her machine. After double-clicking on a few folder icons, she was granted access to the video on the card. She used her wireless mouse to locate a digital needle near the bottom of the video and slid it to the exact time she'd left the office to set up for the poker tournament.

Officer Sherry shook his head. "Isn't that something how things have changed, Dan? I bet when you were on the force, you had to watch a lot of surveillance footage. Did they have this ability to just move to any part of the video within seconds like this?"

"You're right. I did have to watch my fair share.

And no, we had to use VCRs and fast-forward through most of it. If we weren't sure when something happened, we had to sit and watch. Usually, two or three of us would sit and stare at a screen while we mainlined coffee, thinking that was the best way to ensure that we didn't miss anything."

"Welcome to the New Word," Sherry grinned. "Now, Tina was out there for almost forty minutes, so we have a bit of footage to look at, but we'll have a few suspects by the time our couple of hours is up."

Dan caught a glance from Molly out of the corner of his eye.

She had her arms folded and was shaking her head. As interested in this case as he was becoming, he knew there was no way he could allow himself to fully thrust himself into it, nor could he allow Officer Sherry to rope him into yet another wild goose chase around Baldwin Beach.

"Listen, I'd love to help, but I think I'm going to bow out of this investigation," Dan told Sherry. He reached down, held Molly's hand, and slowly pulled her toward the door.

"I'll tell ya what," Sherry mused, not taking his eyes away from the screen. "When we have a list of people, I'll get that to you, and you can zip around here and help me with the interrogations."

"Sounds like a plan." Dan was mildly intrigued

by that as a course of action. However, Molly's newfound death grip on his hand told him that was going to be a hard sell for her as well.

They stepped out of the office and back into the tense evening air, leaving Officer Sherry and Tina to fend for themselves.

15

Stepping out into the evening air was an adjustment for Dan and Molly. The office had been air-conditioned, and the increase by ten degrees, along with the humidity, was almost overwhelming to each of them.

And that was just the air.

The news of the theft had put the participants of the poker night on edge. There was a group of them gathered at the bottom of the office steps. They had formed a human wall, which was growing by the minute as more people caught wind of what was going on and joined the fray, adding extra support to the back side of the barricade.

Dan gave a quick glance at the situation and

decided that the best way to get through the mass of people would be at the edges. People started shouting at them and asking them questions as they came down the steps and made a rush toward the corner of the building and the first *bricks* in the wall.

Their hands were tense and gripped each other like they were connected by super glue. Dan pulled Molly quickly through the fray, and by the time they reached the first person up against the building, they'd already stepped aside, letting Dan and Molly out, giving them a straight, unimpeded walk to their golf cart.

As they jogged over to the cart, they heard a series of hisses and boos come from the mass of people who were crowding the building. They were clearly unhappy with how Dan and Molly had been allowed to go and were taking out their frustration on the kind person at the end of the line.

Both Dan and Molly were thankful for that person's kindness. The thought of what might have happened had that person not let them by formed in each of their minds as Dan put the key in the golf cart and pushed the pedal to the floor.

They drove past the field that had the tables all set up for the tournament less than ten minutes earlier. Now, most of the tables were flipped on their sides, and several of the chairs had been overturned and broken.

Normally, Dan would have just driven to their campsite, but tonight, he thought it might be better to go somewhere else.

16

D own on the beach, a few people had gathered along the seventy-foot bench that had been put in along the sand. It was time to watch the sunset.

Dan put the cart into park, and he and Molly walked up a small composite board ramp onto the beach and found a spot on the bench.

Most of the people who would typically be down here to catch one last marvelous glimpse of the sun for the day were standing in front of the main office of the park, which left plenty of space on the bench for Dan and Molly to have a private moment together.

"What a crazy night," Molly said a few moments

after they sat down. She put her head on Dan's shoulder and heaved a sigh.

"Yeah," Dan echoed her sentiment.

The two sat in silence for a number of minutes, allowing the gentle breeze and sounds of the water lapping up on shore against rocks and sands to rush over them. The sun was slowly descending. Its bright light spread out wondrously over the water and horizon, creating hues of oranges and pinks, purples and blues that were indescribably beautiful and calming — at least to Dan and Molly.

Their taste had soured on this place over the past few months, but these sunsets never seemed to get old.

On many quiet nights, they'd brought their golf cart down here, walked from the sandy parking lot behind a little food truck, down the path to this very bench. Over the months, they'd sat on every part of the bench and admired the setting sun from so many angles. They'd both come to the conclusion that it didn't matter where they sat so long as they were sitting down there by the water.

They had tried to see this majestic glory from their RV site, but the trees were constantly getting in the way of the amazing closing act that the sun and lake put on each and every night. And forget ever seeing something like this back home.

As much as it pained Molly to say it, she whispered to Dan. "You know, there aren't many places we can get something like this. It might actually be worth staying for."

Dan shrugged his shoulder beneath her head. "Why don't we enjoy this one and then make our decision slowly, without so much emotion."

Her heart was full of emotion, and she didn't know how to empty it. She knew he was right, but it bugged her to no end. Especially when everything she was thinking about had to do with her emotional response to the rest of her life.

How could they live happily here? How could she be okay with him constantly being roped into investigations without it driving her crazy and tearing them apart? How could she live the fulfilling and enjoyable retirement she'd dreamt of for years without taking the emotions into consideration?

"We can talk later," she finally said. "But emotions have to be a major part of the discussion. We can't keep pretending that there's an analytical solution to this problem."

Dan sighed. He knew she was right. In his line of work, emotions could get you killed. He had conditioned himself to be machine-like in his thought process — almost robot-like. But even the analytical side of him understood that his wife, and love of his life, needed more from him now.

It broke his heart and filled him with grave concern because he wasn't sure that he would be able to bring enough of himself to the table to fully commit to whatever decision they were eventually going to make.

But he was going to try.

Boy, was he going to try.

17

It was after dark when they finally decided to stand up from the bench and head to their golf cart. The only reason they left that place was because the mosquitos had reached an unbearable level of nuisance, and both of them agreed that scratching bug bites for the next several days just wasn't worth the extra time they were going to have together down by the pitch black beach.

When Dan got into the cart, he noticed his phone was lit up in one of the cup holders.

Picking it up, he said, " Looks like Officer Sherry wants some help on this one."

Molly grabbed the phone from his hands. "Five phone calls in the last two hours?"

She didn't say another word the entire drive back to their RV. She didn't have to.

He had caught all of the subtext from her tone.

It was simple yet direct.

You'd better not return a single one of those calls.

18

The smell of bacon and eggs sizzling enticed Dan to wake up from his slumber. It was a rare occasion that he slept in long enough to smell his wife cooking bacon and eggs, or even making coffee for that matter — but he'd been up later than usual the night before, and the weight of the decision that was looming over them was enough to keep him in bed past his usual early wake-up time.

He lay there with his eyes closed, taking in the smells. The smoky, salty smell of rendering pork belly was one of God's most amazing gifts to humanity, he thought. And though the eggs didn't really smell like much, he could tell they were there. He salivated, almost drooling down the side of his face, thinking about a nice runny yolk bursting out onto his plate, the only solution to clean it up being the piece of bacon in his left hand. Then, wash it all down with a nice swig of steaming black dark roast.

Molly had really done it! She had managed to take his mind off of all of the problems that they were currently embroiled in. He knew that a nice, home-cooked breakfast and perhaps another trip down to the water and they might decide to stay. All he had to do on his end of things was keep out of the danger of the local crime scene.

That was going to be a bit of a challenge, he realized. However, if Molly was willing to get up and cook him breakfast on occasion, that would be a great deterrent from the exploits of his past life.

It didn't have to be every day, either. Dan knew two things. The first was that it was unsustainable for Molly to wake up before he did every day and serve him breakfast. The second being that a diet of bacon and eggs would just be a direct line, albeit slightly slower than the dangers of crime fighting, to an early grave. A retirement filled with clogged arteries, high blood pressure, and a daily pill regiment were not on his list of things to go searching for.

Taking a deep breath, he decided to get up and go hug his wife in the kitchen. He could picture it in his mind. She was standing at the stove. Maybe she was wearing a bathrobe. Maybe she wasn't. He was hopeful that she was. He would slide up behind her and put his head on her shoulder as he wrapped his arms around her.

As soon as he sat up, though, he realized that wasn't going to happen.

Because Molly was still in bed.

She had been the whole time.

19

Perplexed, Dan reached his feet and slowly slid the doorway to their bedroom open. He peered through the small bathroom that led to the kitchen.

With Molly still lying in bed, he wasn't sure what he expected to see. The smell of that beautiful breakfast was close, but there was no smoke nor sign of any of it being prepared in the kitchen.

Slowly, almost gingerly, he stepped through the bathroom and out into the kitchen. He was careful not to step past the refrigerator. Through the small window just above the sink, he could see smoke sailing by outside.

He raised an eyebrow.

That was strange. Who would be cooking out on their front patio?

Dan knew it best not to panic.

He thought about going back into the bedroom and taking a glance out through the window at the foot of the bed but knew that he would risk waking Molly. It would be a shame to do that and get her day started off on the wrong foot if it wasn't necessary. He also didn't want to burst through the sliding screen door with a gun in his hand, pointing it at the trespassing chef. So, he decided on the middle-ground option.

Taking a few more footsteps toward the sink, he could take a glance around the left-hand edge of the window and possibly get a view of whatever was going on out there.

A few more steps, and he was in a position to see who was creating the smoke and where it was coming from.

What Dan discovered was that the smoke was coming from his flat-top griddle. And, indeed, bacon and eggs were the main culprits, but there was also sausage and silver dollar pancakes.

The chef at the helm was the last person he wanted to see.

He rushed toward the front door and slid it open.

"What the heck are doing here?" Dan barked.

"Well, good morning to you, too! I was hungry. We should enjoy some breakfast and have a little chat."

It was clear by the smile on Officer Sherry's face that he was not going to take no for an answer.

20

"You know," Dan said, descending the stairs and walking over to Officer Sherry, "I should call the cops on you."

The two shared a quick smirk.

"I'm here!" Officer Sherry joked, throwing his hands up in the air.

"I'd be lying if I said I wasn't more than a tad uncomfortable with this whole arrangement you've set up here." Dan took a seat at the table and poured himself a cup of coffee from the carafe that Officer Sherry had brought with him.

"I didn't know what kind of coffee you liked," Sherry nodded. "So, I brought a locally roasted blend."

Dan could tell as he was pouring it that it wasn't

his usual dark roast. Thankfully, it wasn't a light roast, either. Medium — he could handle that. And being a cop, he knew that Officer Sherry had brewed it about as strong as humanly possible.

He took a quick swig and noted that it was not his favorite, but it was certainly palatable. A three or four-cup morning was definitely not outside the realm of possibility.

Officer Sherry took a few steps away from the table and picked up the spatula that Dan had routinely hung from the side of his propane gas griddle for years. He glanced at Dan, raised an eyebrow, and flipped the spatula around in his hand a few times in a flourish that would have made Chuck Conners of The Rifleman fame proud. "Pick your poison!"

"It all looks good from where I'm sitting," Dan replied.

The previous evening had been such a letdown at the poker tournament, and he and Molly had spent so much time down by the beach without anything to eat, that he was absolutely famished. Whatever Officer Sherry put on his plate was going to go down, and it was going to go down quickly. And chances were that it would be replaced with a second helping almost as fast.

Sherry threw a heaping helping of pancakes on

one side of the plate. On the other side, he placed a few slices of bacon, a few links of sausage, and two fried eggs.

Setting the plate in front of Dan, he said, "Bon appétit," before loading his plate and grabbing himself a seat at the table.

"This looks delicious," Dan said, reaching for the maple syrup in the middle of the table.

"I try," Officer Sherry feigned humility.

"Now, as smitten as I am with the thought of someone making me a breakfast like this first thing in the morning, I do have to tell you that I would receive it better if it were my wife and not you. So, I have to ask — what the hell are you doing on my porch cooking me breakfast on my griddle?"

Officer Sherry finished smushing a bite of pancake into his mouth. He nodded his head and held up a finger as he reached for his cup of coffee to wash it down and clear some space.

"You know, I knew you were going to ask that question. I could go on some crazy song and dance about how I just really wanted to catch up with you because it had been so long since we'd seen each other. Don't get me wrong — there is some truth to that statement. I've missed you and Molly quite a bit. But the real truth, and the crux of this whole meal has to do with what happened last night with the money at the poker tournament."

Dan dropped his fork and shook his head. "No way. I can't."

He heard the words, *I can't*, as they left his lips. They were weak. Deep down, Dan knew he wanted to. Before Officer Sherry even told him what he had planned for the two of them, and how they were going to saddle up again and go raise some Cain, he knew he wanted in.

But he also knew he was married to Molly, and he loved her. He knew that she was not going to be happy about this new incantation of the same old thing, and he knew that if he were to ride off into the sunset with Officer Sherry having solved yet another crime here at Baldwin Beach RV Resort, that would spell disaster on so many levels. They'd get rid of their place, the trusted bond between husband and wife would be damaged, Dan would never see Officer Sherry again, and if that wasn't bad enough, Dan would have to live out his days at his home in Auburn, sitting across from the woman he'd miffed who would probably hold this decision over his head until the day he died.

It was a lose-lose situation, and he knew it.

But he also knew that there was something within him, a pulling force from way down, that was urging him, coaxing him, to just ask the question and find out what Officer Sherry had in mind for him.

Of course, he knew that asking that question would open a Pandora's Box of trouble for more than just himself.

"Well, I can fully understand your hesitation," Officer Sherry replied, snapping Dan out of his nightmarish hallucination. "But I could really use your help. And trust me, we won't be flying around here in golf carts getting shot at. It would be more office-type work. I figured you could come sit with me at the police station in town and be a second set of eyes on the security footage. That's all."

Just as Dan was entertaining the idea, thinking that it might be a happy compromise that Molly might just actually go for, Molly emerged from the sliding door at the front of the RV.

By the time Dan's gaze went from his plate to her, she had crossed her arms, pursed her lips, and was shaking her head.

"Guess I've got my answer," Officer Sherry sighed. "Would you like some breakfast, Molly?"

21

A s it turned out, Molly was hungry and in the mood for coffee, which wasn't always the case. Oftentimes, she preferred tea in the mornings and early evenings. However, this morning, she was feeling like something a little stronger would be needed.

"So, tell me what you two have been out here cooking up," she said after Officer Sherry had put a plate of food in front of her. She'd poured her own coffee and was drizzling syrup over the top of a couple of flapjacks. "This looks divine, by the way."

"It's really nothing, Molly," Officer Sherry said, sitting back down it his spot. "We've got this missing money from the tournament, and I was just asking

Dan if he would be able to come to the station and be a second set of eyes on the security footage. Nothing dangerous, I promise."

Dan sat next to Officer Sherry in complete silence. His posture and demeanor were more reminiscent of a child whose older sibling was protesting their innocence to an angry mother than that of a retired police officer with over thirty years of protecting the public in his rearview.

"I see," Molly nodded. "And you can assure us that this is not going to lead to any level of risk where my husband's concerned?"

"I'm almost certain he will be completely safe."

"*Almost certain?*"

"Well, you know as well as I do that at Dan's age, he could step out of the shower and fall on his rump and hit his head on the toilet for crying out loud. Or he could step out onto the road to get the mail and get sideswiped by an eighteen-wheeler he never saw coming. So asking me to guarantee a totally risk-free activity isn't really possible. I mean, for all I know, he could sit in the chair a little too long and develop some sort of pelvic or spinal misalignment. You just never, fully, know — you know?"

Molly raised an eyebrow. "You're a strange bird, Officer Sherry."

"I've been told that all my life," he smirked.

Molly's gaze then went to Dan, who was sitting in his chair quietly, drinking his coffee and using a piece of sausage to sop up some of his runny egg yolks. "And this is something you'd like to do?"

Dan shrugged.

Molly shrugged back, making a few facial contortions to mock her once brave husband. "What's this? What in the world does that mean? It doesn't communicate much of anything."

Dan cleared his throat and set his fork down on the edge of his plate, allowing the yolk to overtake the sausage like a tiny boat in a big yellow lake.

"I don't know," he shrugged again. "I think it would be nice to be helpful and try to figure things out."

"Men," Molly shook her head.

"What does that mean?" Officer Sherry butted in. "Does that mean he can do it?"

"No. It means that he's a man. All they ever want to do is solve problems, even when the problem simply requires time and tenderness."

"You think this just requires time?" Officer Sherry was perplexed. "Molly, I'm going to have to go ahead and disagree with you. If we let this go on too long, the thief, whoever they are, will have spent all of the money, and we'll never find out who did it. It was a cash prize, you know, so no real way to track it."

"I wasn't talking about this case," Molly sighed. "I was just speaking of Dan in general. He can't help himself. No matter how many times we say we're not going to do this or do that. No matter how much we say we're not going to get involved, he has to jump right in. He can't not touch things. Those are the ways of the man."

"I think I understand," Sherry nodded. "However, being a man myself, it is quite possible that your woman's logic is lost on me. I'm under the belief that a problem left unaddressed can only stay the same or grow into a larger problem."

"Well, that's what makes the world go around, isn't it? I guess that's why God created man and woman."

Officer Sherry downed the last of his coffee. "You know, Molly, I'd never quite thought about it that way before, but now that you mention it, it certainly makes a lot of sense. Anyway, back to the original question. Can Dan come out to play?"

Molly quickly turned to Dan. "Do you want to?"

Dan kept his eyes on his plate, not once daring to bring them up to meet his wife's, and nodded his head gently.

Molly then turned back to Officer Sherry and said, "Fine. He can go. But on one condition."

"What's that?"

"You'll need a third chair in the room because I'm going, too."

22

They arrived at the police station about forty-five minutes after they finished breakfast. Officer Sherry had graciously cleaned up the mess he'd made on the griddle while Dan and Molly had done the dishes and taken showers.

Dan and Molly opted to take their own car rather than ride with Officer Sherry in the cruiser, just in case they decided that they didn't want to get too involved in the investigation. Having their own vehicle, in their mind, would allow them to pull the plug and leave at any time they wanted.

Dan, however, had a sneaking suspicion that this was one that they were not going to want to leave until they found out who took the money. And the clock was ticking.

Molly, on the other hand, wasn't so sure about the path they were going down on this one. Her involvement was strictly to keep Dan from getting himself involved too deeply.

Officer Sherry invited them into a small room at the end of a thin, dimly lit hallway.

"Pardon the lack of lighting," he apologized, blushing slightly as he opened the door to a small room. It was all set up with three chairs and a laptop computer with a larger monitor sitting on a steel table. There were wires running across the table, along the wall, and into an outlet a few feet away. "We almost never use this room. It's such a small area, and we don't get a ton of crime here. Most of our small little station goes unused to tell you the truth."

"It's fine," Molly assured him as she walked by and took her seat. The chair was hard and cold, prompting a physiological response that sent a shiver through her spine that emanated through her entire body.

Dan took the seat in the middle. Unlike his wife, he was completely unfazed by the cold seat. In fact, given the heat from the sun that had shone through the driver's side window of his car onto his seat, he was relatively relieved to be in a cooler place.

Officer Sherry took his spot at the laptop and

started pressing buttons on the keyboard and getting things set up before he turned on the large monitor.

When the monitor was turned on, a larger version of the laptop's screen came to life and beamed a dull bluish-gray light and slightly grainy image at the three onlookers.

"We've figured out that Tina was out of the office between five-thirty and six-fifteen. That's when she was standing at the front tables helping everyone get registered and showing them to their seats. Skip hadn't been around. He'd told Tina he was going to have a smoke and grab a cart ride until everyone went home for the night."

"Why wouldn't he stick around and help her?" Molly asked.

Officer Sherry shrugged. "I certainly would have, but Skip is what we would lovingly refer to as people averse. Tina didn't think anything of it because it's kind of his M.O. He does this pretty much every time there's a big event. He's always willing to help set up, but the second the campers start gathering, he makes off for hours at a time. Tina knows he's just a text message away if she were to need anything, but by the time she knew she needed something last night, it was too late."

"I'll say," Dan chimed in. "So, we just have to

watch that forty minutes of video and see who was in the place."

"There's a little more to it than that," Officer Sherry narrowed his eyes. "The inside camera is going to give us some information. But it doesn't give us a great view of much besides the back of people. We can't see the safe on it, either. The footage from the outdoor camera will give us a better view of the person's face if they entered the office. But we have no idea what they did inside. So, we're going to be watching both of those. It should take about an hour and a half."

"That's still pretty reasonable," Dan nodded. He'd spent significantly longer portions of his career on the force sifting through video footage where they had no idea what time frame they were working with or what they had even been looking for. Those days were always exhausting and tedious. He recalled more than a few of them where he'd stood up at the end of it, almost unable to feel his legs, and told his fellow footage watchers that he was never doing it again. Of course, crime didn't stop because he wanted it to, and the hours of video watching became a bigger part of his daily detail — especially for the last five or ten years of his career.

Molly shivered and asked, "Do you have anything

warm that I can sip on while we do this? It's quite chilly in here."

"Oh, sure," Officer Sherry said, standing up and heading to the front of the station. He came back a few minutes later with a steaming cup of coffee for Molly. "Sorry about that. I purposely had them cool this room down so that we wouldn't be lulled to sleep while we were watching. This is some truly boring stuff, and if you're not careful, you can miss important details if you allow your mind to drift off to a more comfortable place."

"I see," Molly took a sip. The coffee was not her cup of tea. It was too strong and had a bitter, burned flavor from sitting on the burner for too long. She looked at her watch. It made sense. She often avoided going to the big-name coffee chains after the early morning rush because their coffee takes on the same flavor by late morning or early afternoon. They aren't going to make everything fresh for every customer, and so they let the coffee sit there. Most of the employees are not even coffee drinkers, so they don't know what they're doing to the flavor of the roast — they're just following the policy recommendations from their employee manual.

Nonetheless, she sipped it and allowed the coffee to do the job she'd tasked it with — warming her up. It tasted like crap, but she could deal with the taste in her mouth a lot easier than the cold working its way into her bones.

Now that they were all situated and the first roll of footage was on the screen, Officer Sherry hit the spacebar on the laptop. The numbers at the top of the screen began to move, and they were off, doing the most mind-numbing level of police work ever.

23

During their ninety-minute viewing party, they'd seen seven distinct campers enter the office.

Four of them had been quick in and outs. Less than ten seconds. They had walked into the place, saw Tina wasn't there and then immediately walked out.

Three others, on the other hand, had stayed for anywhere between forty-five seconds and ninety seconds.

"I asked Tina last night if she was sure she'd locked the safe before she went out to help check people in for the tournament," Officer Sherry told Dan and Molly. "She seemed adamant that she had, but looking at this footage, I'm inclined to think that the safe had not been locked properly."

"If it had been locked, in order for that money to be lifted in ninety seconds or less, the thief would have to know the key code prior to entering the office. The clock would be ticking as soon as they walked in."

"You're right." Officer Sherry sat forward and moved his finger along the laptop's finger pad, moving the starting point of the video back a ways. "Do you recognize him?"

Dan and Molly leaned forward and tried to get a good look. After a quick glance at each other, Dan replied, "No, but there are thousands of people at the park. We only know a small handful."

"He's got a backpack," Molly noted.

"That he does," Officer Sherry smirked. He moved his finger along the pad again.

This time, a woman walked into the frame on the right-hand side of the screen and then walked through the bottom left and disappeared from their view.

"Do you see that?" Sherry pointed at a black spot on the bottom of the screen as he brought the video back a few frames. The back of the woman's head was in the bottom of the frame, and there was the smallest black nub of something sticking up from the bottom of the screen just about two inches from where her ponytail dangled.

"Is that a backpack grip?" Dan asked.

"It's hard to tell," Officer Sherry said, squinting at the screen and trying to get a clearer look. "I suppose it's possible that it could be."

Officer Sherry let the footage move forward, and about seventy-five seconds later, the woman walked out, and her head moved from the bottom left of the screen to the middle right. When she walked out, her head moved back and forth a few times. It appeared as though she could have been looking out to see if anyone had seen her go in and out of the office.

"Excuse me." Officer Sherry stood up. "I'll be back in a moment."

Dan and Molly sat in their chairs while Officer Sherry took a brief leave.

"How are you doing?" Dan placed his hand on Molly's arm.

"I'm doing fine. You?"

"Fine."

"Is this type of work filling your desire to stay connected to your law enforcement roots?"

Dan smirked. "I'm glad we could be helpful without all of the risks, but I'd much rather be down by the water enjoying a beer and some sun. If you remember, this was always the part of the job that I hated. Well, this and the seemingly endless piles of forms that had to be completed."

"What do you say we make it a point to head on down to the water when we get back." Molly had taken her free hand and was gliding her index finger over Dan's forearm. "I'd like that very much."

A few moments after he'd left, Officer Sherry came back into the room.

"It won't be long now. I've got Tina coming over to identify these two people with the bags, and then we'll go make a visit."

"I think we've done all that we can do here, Officer Sherry," Molly said, standing up and giving a slight tug on Dan's arm.

Dan stood up, too. "Yeah, I think we're going to head out. You and Tina seem to have a good handle on this."

"Oh," Officer Sherry said. His face looked like that of a seven-year-old who had just learned that his best friend had become best friends with someone else and no longer preferred his company. His eyes wandered from Molly to Dan and then back to Molly as he tried to figure out which one of them was responsible for pulling the rug out from beneath him and abandoning him at this most crucial part of the case. "Are you sure you want to go right now? We're just getting to the good part."

"As much as I have always loved the good part," Dan mused, "I think those days are officially over for me. This was a nice compromise, but I have to be honest — I hate watching security footage. We'll be around."

With that, Dan and Molly turned and left a very stunned and disappointed Officer Sherry by himself in the makeshift office in the dingy back of the Baldwin Beach Police Station.

24

D an and Molly were walking to their car when Molly suggested that they take a quick walk up the street and check out some of the shops on the main drag.

Main Street was about a quarter-mile walk away and Dan hadn't had his daily walk yet, so it was actually a perfect little plan.

They enjoyed the better part of two hours, popping into shop after shop. Most of them were nothing to write home about and Dan had no interest in things like trinkets and knickknacks. He definitely had no use for natural soaps and essential oils or books on how to make your own. But this excursion meant the world to Molly. She was happier than he'd seen her in a long time, and he was enjoying the time with her. It was fun to watch her pick things up and study them. He noted the items that she held onto the longest, thinking that maybe when Christmas rolled around, he'd make the drive up and pick some of them up.

That seemed like it might be a bit of a stretch, so he began thinking of a way to save himself a three-hour round trip on snow-covered roads. Then it hit him — he would come out tomorrow while Molly was sleeping and buy some of her more desired items. He was sure he could find a way to hide them. Of course, if she found them, it wasn't really a big deal either. He knew, no matter if they made it until Christmas or not, he was going to get a big smooch out of the deal for being so thoughtful. Heck, it might even be in the cards that he could get one of Molly's amazing back scratches.

There really was nothing quite as pleasing as lying down on his bed, a pillow tucked beneath the side of his face, while he drifted off to sleep because of the feeling of Molly's amazing nails lightly dragging along the length of his back. It was as good as life on earth got — a veritable Heaven before Heaven came.

After they'd finished looking through the shops, they tried a little diner in town that they'd both been told about by some of the folks at the RV resort. People raved about this place, and for good reason.

For less than thirty dollars, they had their fill, and it was the most delicious meal they'd had in a while. Dan had a bowl of broccoli cheddar soup to start and then a Shrimp Po Boy sandwich with thick-cut steak fries that were crispy on the outside and fluffy white on the inside. The creole seasoning that was used in the sandwich on the shrimp was also lightly dusted on the fries just after they'd come out of the fryer, creating a harmony in the dish that Dan appreciated.

Molly had a bowl of the seafood bisque, which was creamy and salty and just out of this world. She followed that up with a shaved beef salad with white balsamic vinaigrette.

The two of them left the place stuffed and smiling, ready to head back to their camp for a nap and then a trip down to the water for the evening.

As they walked to their car, both of them thought that Baldwin Beach was a truly beautiful place with some great shops and amazing food. The sunsets were worth the price of admission. If they could live a simple life and stay away from crime, this would be a place they would definitely enjoy for a few months out of the year.

25

The evening came and went, and the sunset wasn't enjoyed by Dan and Molly. They had arrived home around four, and both of them laid down to take a nap, but both of them slept through the night until the following morning.

Dan was awoken at eight O'clock by a knock on the door of their RV.

He stumbled through, rubbing the sleep from his eyes and bouncing from side to side, his hips and the walls guiding him to the front door.

His clothes from the day before were hanging on him, and he could still smell Po Boy sandwich and fried food on them.

Opening the door, he shielded his eyes from the sun that was making its way into the place.

Officer Sherry was standing on the porch and Tina was down at the bottom of the stairs looking upward.

"Wow," Sherry said when Dan opened the door. "You look like Hell."

"What time is it?"

"After eight."

Dan nodded, trying to get his body to straighten up. He was exhausted, though, and could have used another couple of hours in bed.

"What are you doing here?" He asked Officer Sherry.

"So, we've got some information about the case. I was hoping Tina and I could come in and share the details so you and Molly can be on the lookout."

"No," Dan shook his head. "Sorry, I'm officially retired. You two are going to have to do this work if you want it done."

"Aw, come on. You can't convince me that you don't want in on this. All we need you to do is let us know if you've seen the two people we've identified as the thieves."

"Why don't you just go to their site? They're bound to show up there eventually."

"They haven't been there in a few days. At least that's what their neighbors told Tina when she stopped by last night."

"Okay? So, keep going there until they show up? Or look up their home residences in the system and send an officer out to bring them in for questioning."

"They're from out of state," Sherry said. The look on his face was grave. "I'm telling you, Dan, they're somewhere around here, and we're going to need all the help we can get to snuff them out."

"*Snuff them out?*"

Sherry raised an eyebrow. "You're not familiar with that term?"

"Of course, I'm familiar with the term. Don't you think it sounds a little severe for a couple of amateurs who happened to wander into the office and put some money in their backpacks?"

"Nobody's seen them since that night," Tina finally piped up. Her voice was soft and insecure. "They've been missing for almost forty-eight hours. With that kind of money on their person, I think they might be in serious danger."

Dan closed his eyes and leaned against the sliding door. "Missing doesn't necessarily mean danger. If they have a whole lot of extra cash, it's quite possible they could be out spending it and having a great time."

"Their car is still in their lot," Tina said.

"Have you been inside the RV?" Dan asked. "You must have enough cause for a warrant."

Officer Sherry shook his head and crossed his arms. "Listen, Dan. I know you're looking for an easy way to have this situation resolved, but it's just not going to. We have been in the RV. We looked for the bag and the money. We looked for the two people on the video. They are nowhere to be found. Their car is at the site. Their wallets, purses, and IDs were on the counter. The golf cart keys were there, too. The fridge was full of food, and they had a suitcase full of clothes in the bedroom. They've either taken refuge somewhere in the park, or someone took exception with them, and they're currently in a whole heap of trouble—" Officer Sherry stopped and looked up at Dan, the most serious of looks in his eyes. "That's if they're even still alive at all."

"I'd love to help," Dan said. "But I'm finished with this kind of thing. I'm sorry."

He took a step back and shut the door, locking it and drawing a set of sliding curtains in front of it.

Sitting down in his chair, he waited for Officer Sherry and Tina to leave before he started rocking and gnawing at his thumb nail.

26

It was another few hours before Molly rose from her slumber. Dan hadn't moved from his rocking chair, and his thumb was red and sore from the damage he'd inflicted on himself.

He thought Officer Sherry and Tina were probably jumping to some pretty crazy conclusions about the whereabouts of the two people with the backpacks. It was possible that they were just out on a shopping spree somewhere. It was also possible that they had merely crashed at a friend's site while they waited for the dust to settle before coming out and going about their daily lives as though nothing had happened and no money had ever been taken from the main office safe.

Their car was still parked at their own place and

hadn't moved in several days. With all of the online options available to people, it was completely possible that they had gotten themselves an online driver to take them to a remote location somewhere until everyone forgot that they'd ever been at Baldwin Beach RV Resort.

All of these things were possible.

Dan knew as much.

But there was something deep in his gut, a feeling that he'd had many times before. It was a feeling that one didn't easily forget or dismiss. It was the dreaded feeling that something about this situation was certainly off and that there just wasn't any way it was ever going to sit right without further investigation.

Knowing this filled Dan with dread. He was trying so hard not to get involved. He knew that Molly would have none of this, and he could feel her presence right behind him. Guilt for even thinking these thoughts began pushing its way inside of his soul.

Her hand came to rest on his shoulder. It was soothing and menacing all at the same time. A confession was imminent. There was no way he could feel the way he was feeling and not let her know about it. And there was no way he could hide it from her. Over the years, she had become every bit a detective of his heart — the best detective there ever was.

"I know," she said. Her voice was soft and soothing, without even the slightest hint of judgement or frustration. "I'll be right there by your side. We'll help with this one, and then we leave here forever."

He sat silently, his rocking in the chair, stopping for the first time since he'd sat down.

As if she could read his every thought, she continued. "I'll shower, we'll zip around on the cart and see what we can find, and then we'll come back here, pack up our things, and head home. We'll list this place, and we can spend the next few weeks figuring out how we're both going to get what we want out of retirement."

There was no response from Dan except for the lowering of his shoulders and the tension leaving his body.

With that, Molly took her hand off his shoulder and headed back to the shower, leaving Dan with many things to sort out.

27

The morning air was cool on their faces as Dan and Molly sped through the park on their golf cart. Neither one of them was sure what they were looking for, but they knew it was going to be something abnormal — which actually was normal for this place.

Abnormal definitely wouldn't be hard to find. Figuring out which abnormal was the abnormal they were supposed to investigate further…that was going to be the challenge.

Their first stop was the main office.

They found Tina at the computer and Officer Sherry perched on a stool behind her. They were pouring over the security footage again, but this time, it wasn't for the main office. It was for many of the other areas of the park.

As soon as Dan and Molly stepped into the office, Sherry stood up and smiled. "I knew you couldn't stay away." He walked over to Dan and grabbed his hand in an aggressive shake. Then, he stepped back and saluted him. "Happy to have you aboard, sir!"

Dan didn't return his enthusiasm. "Don't get too excited. Lord knows I'm not. Officer Sherry, this is officially my last case." He turned to Tina. "Tina, sweet as you are, we will be selling our camper, and we won't be re-leasing our site for next year."

Tina frowned. "Oh, that's so sad. I really liked you two. You seemed so normal compared to some of these other folks. And reasonable. You never bother anyone or ask for anything."

"Well," Molly interjected, "That's part of the problem for us, I guess. We really don't fit in here. It was a nice place to visit, and we'll have…interesting memories. But this is not our home away from home, I'm afraid."

"Understood," Officer Sherry chimed back in. "Well, since this is our last hurrah, let's make it count!"

Dan smiled weakly. "Not too much, okay? I don't want to leave here in an ambulance or a hearse."

"Bah," Officer Sherry scoffed at Dan's concerns.

"You'll be fine. You always are. I bet they called you Teflon Dan when you were on the force, didn't they?"

"Actually, they called me *By the Book, Dan*."

Officer Sherry, who'd been making his way back to his perch, stopped dead in his tracks and turned his head slowly back to Dan. "Really? That's so sad."

Dan shrugged. "It's so true. There's a reason I made it through my entire career without issue. Most of it was due to God's grace. The other part of it was because I did things the right way."

Molly wrapped her arm around Dan's and hugged him. "I'm so thankful for both."

"Well, here's what we've got," Sherry said, pointing at the screen. "We've got this fella dumping large quantities of mulch where he shouldn't be dumping. Tina says his name is Bill, something or other."

"Dodge," Tina added quickly.

"Yeah. Bill Dodge. He's a retired history teacher. Truth be told, I've only met him a handful of times, but the fact that a school district hired this guy to work with peoples' children is beyond scary. Mouth that would make a trucker blush and a drinking habit to boot."

Dan raised an eyebrow. "I think we've met him before. That name sounds familiar." He moved around the desk and took a glance at the screen. "Oh yeah. That's the guy."

Molly followed and nodded. "Yup. We met him and his wife the other night before the tournament was supposed to begin. They were quite the pair."

"Well, he's become something of a post-retirement mowing and landscaping service around here." Officer Sherry crossed his arms and paused for a second.

Dan asked, "So what does this guy have to do with the two people who were caught on camera in the office with backpacks? I thought we were looking for them. Not some guy who's dumping mulch where he shouldn't be."

Tina piped up. "It's a bit of a hunch, and I'm not quite sure there's any merit to it, but when I was asking around the park if anyone had seen the two missing people, several of them told me that they'd overheard an argument between them and Bill recently. They said it had gotten really heated, and he had threatened them, saying that if they didn't come up with some money soon, he was going to kill them."

"He said that out in the open?" Dan asked. He was beyond surprised that someone would make such a bold threat out loud in a place like this. For Heaven's sake, it seemed like sometimes people around could hear him fart in the shower. The last thing he would do was go around making murder threats — even at a whisper level.

"So, he's a bit of a drinker," Tina nodded. "He says lots of things when he gets good and liquored up."

"A lot of people do that," Molly chimed in. "It doesn't mean they remember them the next morning. And most of them never carry through with them."

"Well, Bill's a little different." Officer Sherry unfolded his arms and went over to a small red binder on the counter next to the safe. He pulled the binder and opened it up. "May I?" He asked Tina.

"Be my guest."

"This, here, is the complaints binder. Tina and Skip will share it with me periodically. It holds all of the formal complaints made about campers in the resort. Now, most of these never make it to a point where I would have to get involved, but Tina likes me to know about things that might lead to an escalated situation. I usually check this about once a week while I'm over here.

"It has all sorts of different things. Minor trespassing, using inappropriate language in front of peoples' kids, drinking too much, driving too fast with the golf carts, monopolizing the horseshoe pits — things of that nature."

Dan nodded. "Let me guess, Bill shows up in that book quite a bit."

"A whole lot," Sherry nodded.

"That doesn't mean he had anything to do with the disappearance of our thieves."

"No, it doesn't. But most of the complaints in here about him stemmed from threats he made while he was drunk. Listen to this one: Bill Dodge threatened to ride his golf cart through one of the camper's yards after a rain storm because he failed to pay for services rendered."

"Did he do it?" Molly asked.

"Yes, he did. Made one hell of a mess, too."

"And he got away with it?"

"The tenant never went to the police about it. Only discussed the threat with Tina, but after the deed had been done — nothing. Not a peep."

"Read them the one about the bushes," Tina encouraged.

"Bushes?" Molly asked.

"Bushes." Officer Sherry nodded. "It seems Bill is very sensitive when someone criticizes his landscaping abilities. This person, who resides in camp 1254, had their bushes planted by Bill. The job was done poorly — says here it was rushed — and he complained to Bill one night. Of course, Bill was drunk and said if he didn't like the work, then he'd personally stop by and pee all over the bushes for the next few weeks, which would kill them dead."

"We've driven past that RV," Dan nodded. "Every time we go past there, Molly comments about what a shame it is that they put all that money into those shrubs, and now they're dying. We had no idea Bill was murdering them."

"Afraid so," Officer Sherry nodded. "I actually paid this fella a visit, but he clammed right up. Refused to speak and asked me to leave. Apparently, he's more afraid of what Bill could be capable of if he were angered further. Dead bushes were enough to scare poor 1254 off."

"Alright," Dan began, walking over to the book that Officer Sherry was holding onto. He took the book and gave it a quick glance. "So, Bill Dodge is a real piece of work who makes life miserable for people around here. He's done nothing that anyone is willing to call the police about, and yet he's now suspected of killing these thieves. Do we even know who the thieves are?"

"Oh yeah," Tina said. "Let me pull up their files."

28

Robby and Cindy Lemmock were the thieves' names. They had been residents for only a short time. Tina told them as she clicked open their file on her laptop.

"They had a reputation for being very kind but always down on their luck. They weren't site owners here like you. They rented an RV and parked in the guest sites. They had signed up for a two-month stay at the beginning of the spring."

"What was your opinion of them?" Dan asked.

"Oh, I thought they were sweet. A nice couple from out of state, just trying to get away from things for a little while. Honestly, they reminded me of you. They were both newly retired, trying to find their footing in that world of workless days."

"I met them a few times, too, but never got to know their names." Officer Sherry said. "When we were watching the camera footage the other day, it never dawned on me that I had seen them before, but after talking with Skip about things, I remembered who they were."

"Skip knew them?" Molly asked.

"Oh yeah," Tina laughed. "They were always in here complaining about things not working properly. Skip was practically a third resident in their camper for the first month they were here. If I didn't know Skip better, I'd say he might be the one who had threatened to kill them and then carried it out. He would see them coming and get so frustrated. They were up his rear end for sure."

"Okay," Dan said, furrowing his brow. "So, why, if they could afford to rent a site here for months in the summer, would they need to steal the cash for the poker tournament?"

"That's a good question," Officer Sherry asked. "Tina, would you care to let them in on the goods?"

"The way it works here," Tina took over, "is that you pay the first half of your visit up front and the last half of your visit at the end of the first week of your stay."

Molly raised an eyebrow. "That is the strangest thing I've ever heard."

"Tell me about it," Tina nodded. "Trust me, it's nothing I made up. It came from corporate. Makes bookkeeping mighty challenging, I can attest to that."

"So, they were able to pay for the first half of their stay, I'm assuming," Dan interjected. "But I'm guessing there was a snag on the last half."

"Correct," Tina nodded. "Turns out they had some issue with their home that wasn't working out, and they'd hired a lawyer who pretty much wiped out their life savings in a matter of months. At least that was the story that Cindy told me when she was in here last."

"It only took months to wipe out their life savings?" Molly mused. "You've got to be kidding me. How in the world did they manage to retire?"

"If you ask them, everything was amazing. It was great until you pressed them on financial issues. Once you needed money for anything, or you said something was going to cost them money to fix, they would clam up and retreat into their camper, and we wouldn't see them for days. They were a strange pair, and Skip couldn't wait to get rid of them."

"Hold on a minute!" Dan chimed. "Let me guess — Bill Dodge mowed the site for them, didn't he?"

"Bingo," Officer Sherry said.

"Let me see that book again," Dan said, reaching out for the binder. He flipped a few pages in and saw a complaint made almost six weeks earlier by Bill Dodge about campers at a temporary site who were refusing to pay him for his services. It says here he'd mowed three times and gotten nothing."

"Well, that doesn't mean he killed them for crying out loud," Molly argued.

"No," Officer Sherry said. "It doesn't. But the cameras we've been monitoring around the park have given us insight into a very different routine in the way Bill dumps his clippings."

"What do you mean?" Dan asked.

"He used to take them over to a little marsh. We gave him permission to dump there any time as long as it was daylight," Tina informed them. "However, during the last two nights, he's taken loads over the garbage dumpster late at night."

"That is something," Dan nodded. "Seems to me that if he was making multiple trips to the dumpster over the course of a few days, he's trying to make it look like he's not doing anything wrong. The fact that it's taking as long as it is means he might still have remnants of Robby and Cindy at his place if he did what you're suggesting he did."

"That was my thought exactly," Officer Sherry nodded. He turned to Molly. "I hope you don't mind, but I'd love to take your husband with me and go pay this Bill Dodge a visit."

Molly stuck a finger in Officer Sherry's face. "This is the last time, and you make sure you bring him home safe and sound."

"I promise I will do my best to make sure that not a hair on his head is out of place when we come back to you."

29

Dan and Officer Sherry loaded up in the Baldwin Beach Police Cruiser, leaving Tina and Molly together in the office, and headed down the narrow RV-lined road.

"You know," Dan thought aloud, "we could probably just go check the dumpster for bits of body parts if we wanted. Then we could go to Bill's site if we need to."

"I wish we could do that, but the garbage is picked up at seven sharp every morning. This is our best bet if we want to nab the bugger today."

They drove in anticipation of the showdown that was imminent. Bill had proven himself to be loud and boisterous. He was a large man with a great deal of strength. Not to mention, despite what the words coming from his mouth were, he was incredibly intelligent.

A small knot in Dan's stomach formed the closer they got to Bill's site. He knew this was his last adventure of this sort. The excitement that he'd felt so many times before, along with his love for the work had left him. He thought back to a conversation he'd had with his ninety-five-year-old neighbor, Richard. Richard had told him that there would come a day when the career he had left would finally let go of him. For Richard, it had happened suddenly. He'd just woken up one day and laid in bed for an extra hour, realizing he didn't have to get up and go to the office. Richard told Dan that he hung out in his boxer shorts all day that day — just because he could.

Dan couldn't help but think that he was experiencing that moment as they made their way to a potential murderer's residence. His desire to 'catch the bad guy' was gone. All he wanted to do was jump out of the cruiser, run back to Molly, grab their things, and go.

It wasn't a feeling of cowardice. He knew that he was willing to face down any threat that came his way, and he knew that if Bill had done what they suspected him of, that he was willing to do the right thing to get him away from law-abiding citizens and put him where he belonged.

So, he wasn't afraid.

He was tired.

He was old.

And he was just flat-out done with this life.

Over the years, it had become a joke between him and Molly that she always came to her senses before he did. Dan always thought he was right. But over time, he would learn that Molly had been the correct one all along. This played into almost every aspect of his life. His faith, their money, and their lifestyle decisions. Molly always seemed to be a few years ahead of him. And God bless her because she was patient enough for him to work through his mental hurdles. She'd watched him struggle through things that, in hindsight, had seemed so clear and simple, yet he'd held onto his old ways and made Molly wait even longer.

This was another one of those situations. Molly knew he should have been done with all of this a long time ago. She'd urged him to stop, given him many reasons why he should, and sat back and watched him as he continued to go out on one wild goose chase after another.

Officer Sherry put the cruiser into park and killed the engine.

Dan looked out the window at the camper with the impeccable lawn and the shrubbery that was freshly mulched.

Bill's truck was parked next to his golf cart, loaded with all of his mowers, weed eaters, shovels, and other tools of his trade.

"If we get out of here alive," Dan sighed, "I am never doing this again."

"Lost your zeal?" Officer Sherry joked.

"Something like that."

"Well then, let's go make this one count."

30

They stepped out of the cruiser tentatively, Officer Sherry with his hand rested on his gun next to his hip, Dan sidestepping his way down the side of the truck, taking his place behind Officer Sherry as he made his way toward the front of the place.

In the front yard, a mulch-hauling side-by-side utility vehicle was parked.

They approached it and noticed that it had been recently hosed down. There were bits of drying mulch on the ground next to it, and clusters of flies were buzzing around them.

"Have you ever seen flies cluster around mulch like this before?" Officer Sherry smirked at Dan.

"Not unless there's some other kind of organic

material mixed in with it," Dan returned. "You ever known someone to hose down the bed of their side by side like this before?"

"Only if they're putting it away for the season," Sherry offered. "But there's still months of mowing and landscaping season left around here."

"My thoughts exactly."

A shift in the wind occurred. It would have gone unnoticed had they been at any other site in the place. It was so subtle, and might have simply been thought of as refreshing as it blew through. But this wind brought forth a rancid smell. It was a smell that Dan had experienced a few times in his long career. The smell of decaying flesh was one that a person never forgets, and that smell was coming from Bill's RV with the gentle breeze.

Dan gagged, and Officer Sherry threw up on the ground beside the side-by-side.

"What are you doing on my lawn?" The sound came out loud and slurred as Bill emerged from the front door, holding a bottle of beer and a shotgun.

Officer Sherry regained his composure and stood up.

"Put the gun down," Sherry yelled. "We're here to talk."

"I bet you're here to talk. That's how it always goes. You come and talk, and then there's a shootout, and someone always goes to jail. This used to be a free friggin' country. Now it's the land of Big Brother."

"Bill Dodge put the gun down and step outside." Officer Sherry's voice had changed. He wasn't conversational. He was commanding.

Dan stood at the side, his body rigid and exposed.

"I'm not coming out there to talk with you. You're here to arrest me, ain't ya?"

"We need to ask you some questions," Officer Sherry replied. "Come outside and leave the gun inside."

Bill looked off to his left behind the door and handed the gun off. Dan could see a woman's arm reach out and take it.

"If these two try to put cuffs on me," Bill instructed, "you come out and shoot them, okay?"

He then took a swig from his beer and stepped down onto the patio.

"Now, what the hell is this all about?"

"We have reason to believe that you have murdered two campers, Robby and Cindy Lemmock."

"I can't believe this! This is absolutely bull! I didn't kill anyone. Especially those two losers! Why would I kill them? Can you tell me that? Why would I kill them?"

"I'm not in the business of the why, sir," Officer Sherry said. "I'm more focused on the if. We've seen you on camera dumping your mulch and clippings in the dumpster the last few nights, which was not the arrangement you'd made with the front office. We also have records of you threatening to kill Robby and Cindy publicly for refusing to pay you for services rendered. Your side-by-side has been recently hosed off—"

"Hosing off a side by side is a crime now?! You two are a friggin' joke." He took a step towards them. Officer Sherry pulled his pistol from his holster and pointed it at the ground just in front of Bill's feet.

"Take one step closer, and I will shoot your toes off. You stay right where you are until we're finished talking."

Bill stopped and dropped his beer before crossing his arms. "You haven't got the cajones to shoot me. You're just as yellow as every other cop around this nation. They like to pick on the little guy while the real criminals go free."

"As I was saying," Officer Sherry continued, ignoring Bill. "There are flies swarming around the bits of mulch on the ground, and the smell from the back of your camper is very recognizable as rotting flesh. That's more than enough for me to obtain a warrant to search the premises. If I were you, I'd make it easy on yourself and just allow us to do our jobs and take a look."

"Honey!" Bill yelled. "Now!"

Bill's wife, Sandra, emerged from her hiding place and pointed the shotgun at Officer Sherry.

Dan dove to his right as she pulled the trigger on the shotgun. He heard a second shot as he watched Officer Sherry dive to his left.

A bullet ripped through Sandra's knee, and she dropped the shotgun to the ground. The shot from her gun missed Officer Sherry and hit the side panel of the side-by-side. Pieces of buckshot scattered and ricocheted off the vehicle. Several of them hit Bill in the legs and dropped him fast.

He lay on the ground screaming and wailing. Sandra let out a shriek from the camper as Dan got to his feet and charged. The woman tried to reach for the shotgun despite the bullet wound on her leg.

Dan was able to get to it before she could and grabbed it.

Officer Sherry stood up and limped over to Bill, who was holding his leg. There were several little popcorn kernel-sized holes just above his knee in the fatty part of his flesh.

"Those'll heal in the next few days," Sherry said, offering Bill a hand up.

"Go screw yourself," Bill grunted through a grimace.

"I think I'll arrest you for the murders of Robby and Cindy Lemmock, plus assaulting a police officer and resisting arrest. Those wounds won't scab over nearly as quickly as the buckshot to the leg."

He pulled out his handcuffs and shoved Bill over on his side so he could cuff the man's hands behind his back.

"Do you have a spare set of cuffs," Dan asked. "I'll go get her cuffed up."

"Glove box of the cruiser," Officer Sherry nodded.

Dan retrieved them and handcuffed Sandra, who had just about passed out and offered no resistance.

It was all Dan could do to keep his stomach contents down. The smells of burning candles, potpourri, and rotting bodies filled the entirety of the camper.

He had no idea how two people could live in such a mess, but it was clear that they felt desperate about it. Sandra was clearly afraid of Bill, and Dan was sure that he'd told her it was just for a short amount of time until he could get rid of both Robby and Cindy.

"Hey," Officer Sherry asked as he pulled Bill up

to his feet. "Why did you kill them? It wasn't just because they didn't pay you for your services, was it?"

"Naw," Bill scoffed. "They stole from me, but they also stole from the park. I watched 'em do it. Then they had the nerve to try to pay me with their stolen money. I knew someone had to do something about these damn criminals running around here. So, while you were off somewhere hiding, not doing your duty, I took the law into my own hands."

"It seems you have a very keen sense of justice, sir," Officer Sherry shook his head. "Well, taking two lives for a relatively small sum of money is going to cost you more than an afternoon of unrewarded work. You're going to go away for a good long time."

"Typical cop," Bill grunted. "Always taking out the righteous guy who's just trying to make the place a little better."

"Interesting perspective," Sherry nodded. "I think you may have spent too many years listening to fifteen-year-olds argue about the events of history. It seems to have taken away all of your wisdom and given you a warped version of the world you live in."

"You're lucky I'm in handcuffs, or I'd kick your fanny all over this park and charge people to watch."

Officer Sherry gave Bill a shove toward the cruiser and called to Dan. "I think we just added an additional charge of threatening an officer to this guy's rap sheet, didn't we?"

"He should know that he's got the right to remain silent," Dan smiled as he got Sandra to her feet and helped her out of the camper and down the steps. "Of course, that's probably true only in the movies."

Once they'd gotten the married criminals into the back of the cruiser and called an ambulance to come look at their wounds, Officer Sherry asked, "So, you're really leaving this place?"

"Really leaving," Dan nodded. "This isn't me anymore. It was once, but I've got to move and leave this behind. And after this case, I can tell you it won't be hard for me. I'm ready to be done. You'll understand someday."

"Well, that's a shame. I like having you around. And watching you jump out of the way when she fired that shotgun was something else. You've still got it."

"Maybe," Dan shrugged. "But that jump used to take me a day to recover from. I'll be struggling with every breath for the next two weeks because of that now. It's time for me to accept what we all eventually must. Time is passing me by, and my time for these types of things is over. I have to move on and live the last third of my life. It's been a lot of fun getting to know you, though. And I hope we can stay in touch. You're a great cop."

Officer Sherry looked away, not wanting to get caught up in the emotion of the moment. "That means a lot coming from you. I appreciate it."

Then, as if overtaken by a force he couldn't explain, Sherry turned and gave Dan a hug.

"Aw, isn't that sweet!" Bill mocked them from inside the cruiser. "A couple of tough guys getting in touch with their inner woman."

Officer Sherry just shrugged.

"Are you sure you want to leave all this behind?"

"One hundred percent."

31

The poker tournament was back on and would be taking place the next day. By the time the adventure and mystery of everything was all over, Dan and Molly had agreed to stay one more night.

They took in one last sunset, knowing that it was going to be an aspect of this place that they were surely going to miss.

On the way back to their site, they saw flyers that had been posted on trees and light poles while they were down enjoying their time by the beach. The prize money from the last tournament was long gone, and there was no way to bill the tournament as an opportunity to win the massive prizes.

So, Tina and Skip had done the next best thing.

It was a pay-to-play affair, with half of the prize money going to a local charity, and the other half going to the winner. It was a great idea and probably one that they should have employed with the first incantation of the tournament.

Nonetheless, Dan and Molly had completely lost interest in this place, and no amount of poker, prize money, or charity donation could get them to stay. They could play poker at home, they didn't need the prize money, and they both handsomely supported a number of charities and causes that they were quite fond of.

The next morning, the two allowed themselves to sleep in and enjoy the camper one last time. They had a leisurely breakfast and took long showers. Dan sat in his rocking chair on the patio and burned the propane fire one last time. Molly sat in her chair and read a cheesy romance novel. Then, they grilled up some hot dogs and enjoyed one last cookout.

That was enough. They'd gotten it out of their system, and both of them knew they were making the right decision.

After Dan and Molly had packed up their things and were heading out, they noticed that Tina and Skip were in the process of setting up poker tables, and they'd hired a company to come cater the gathering. They were moving in their trucks to get everything just so before the contestants made their way to the field for a very different tournament than they'd experienced a few days earlier.

"Hey!" Tina shouted when she saw their car. She flagged them down and ran into the road, forcing them to stop.

Molly rolled down her window, and Dan put the car into park. Tina went around to Molly's side and peered into the vehicle. "You guys sure you don't want to stay and see if you can help us raise some money? I heard you're pretty good at this game?"

"We appreciate the offer," Dan said politely. He didn't want to stay long. He was ready to go if that was to be their path. Long, drawn-out goodbyes were definitely not his thing.

"Well, we're gonna miss you," Tina said.

"Likewise," Molly nodded. "But sometimes, you've got to know when it's time to fold."

"Well played," Tina gave a thumbs up and backed away from the car. "Drive safely."

Molly rolled up the window and she and Dan took off, leaving Baldwin Beach RV Resort for the last time, driving into the sunset of the rest of their lives.

AFTERWORD

Dear Readers,

Thank you so much for reading through the RV Resort Mysteries Series.

Over the past three books, I've really grown to love Dan and Molly. That's why I've made the difficult decision that this will be their last mystery.

Where they go from here, I have no idea — but that's no longer up to me.

I could have continued to put them through hell, making up all sorts of terrible situations in the resort. But I don't want them to live that life.

And yes, I am aware that they are only made-up characters in my crazy little stories, but when you spend time with these characters day in and day out, you find yourself becoming connected to them in some strange way.

I wanted more for them.

And I realized that for them to continue to go through the cozy mystery motions it would eventually destroy their marriage and crush the dreams of their retirement. Any sane couple would walk away from the place they'd tried to call their 'home away from home.'

And so, Dan and Molly, being the sane couple that they are, have decided to walk (or drive) away from the place that has caused them a great deal of stress and danger.

Honestly, I can't say I blame them.

Thank you so much for choosing to read my words. I am so blessed to have readers like you who care about these stories almost as much as I do!

God Bless,
Maisy
September, 2023

ALSO BY MAISY MARPLE

Connie Cafe Series

Coffee & Corpses

Ligature & Latte

Autumn & Autopsies

Pumpkins & Poison

Death & Decaf

Turkey & Treachery

Mistletoe & Memories

Snow & Sneakery

Repairs & Renovations

Bagels & Bible Study

S'more Jesus

Proverbs & Preparations

Books & Bookings

Sharpe & Steele Series

Beachside Murder

Sand Dune Slaying

Boardwalk Body Parts

Fun in the Sun

Out to Sea

RV Resort Mystery Series

Campground Catastrophe

Bad News Barbecues

Sunsets and Bad Bets

Fun Foodie Mysteries

Burger & Dies

Died Shrimp

Ice Scream Sundae

Pastor Brown Series

O Holy Night

A Time to Repent

Trials of the Heart

Bite-Size Mystery

Christmas Murder in July

Dye-ing to Know

Short Stories

Forty Years Together

Long Story Short

The Best Gift of All

Miracle at the Mall

The Ornament

The Christmas Cabin

Cold Milk at Midnight

Coffee on Christmas

The Inn

Merry Little Christmas

Away in a Manger

A Christmas to Remember

Alone in the Woods

Short Story Collections

2021 Christmas Short Story Challenge

2022 Christmas Short Story Challenge

Addiction Help

Hard Truths: Overcoming Alcoholism One Second At
A Time

GET THREE FREE STORIES!

Click the banner to get three free stories!

ABOUT THE AUTHOR

Maisy Marple is a lover of small-town cozy mysteries, plus she has a wicked coffee habit to boot. She loves nothing more than diving into a clean mystery with a cup of the darkest, blackest coffee around.

She grew up in a small town and now lives in the country, giving her more than enough inspiration for creating the cozy locales and memorable characters that are on display in her Connie Cafe Mystery Series!

Also, she hates social media — so you won't find her there.

To connect with Maisy, sign up for her VIP reader list and get a free mystery story. Check out the offer on the previous page.

Made in the USA
Columbia, SC
29 September 2023

23588309R00095